The Chemist Who
Lost His Head

Frontispiece. Portrait of Antoine and Marie Lavoisier by Jacques-Louis David, 1788. Mme. Lavoisier's portfolio of drawings on the chair in the background may be seen as a reminder by David that his onetime pupil had ability as an artist.

The Chemist Who Lost His Head

The Story of
Antoine Laurent Lavoisier

VIVIAN GREY

Coward, McCann & Geoghegan, Inc.
New York

Published simultaneously in Canada by
General Publishing Co. Limited, Toronto.
Designed by Linn Fischer
First printing
Printed in the United States of America

Library of Congress Cataloging in Publication Data

Grey, Vivian. The chemist who lost his head.
Bibliography: p.
Includes index.
Summary: Recounts the life of the French chemist whose work helped transform
many of the undocumented scientific beliefs of the Middle Ages into an exact science.
1. Lavoisier, Antoine Laurent, 1743-1794—Juvenile literature. 2. Chemists—France—
Biography—Juvenile literature.
[1. Lavoisier, Antoine Laurent, 1743-1794. 2. Chemists] I. Title.
QD22.L4G73   540′.92′4   [B]   [92]   82-1571   AACR2
ISBN 0-698-20559-6

For My Daughters
Leslie
and Jackie
And for Mom
With Love

Acknowledgments

I am indebted to the archivists and researchers, for the material in this book is taken from official records and from conversations with scientists and historians. I also owe a debt of gratitude to the chemists and teachers of science for their patient cooperation and interest in this project. And lastly, I thank Refna Wilkin, whose editorial judgment stood in good stead from first to last.

V.G.

Contents

One

ANTOINE LAURENT LAVOISIER was on trial for his life. No one could have been more surprised at what was happening.

His whole world was turning upside down. He was a famous chemist, not a criminal. And yet on this morning of May 8, 1794, he was standing in a Paris courtroom defending himself against charges that involved his very life.

It was all the more surprising because of his worldwide reputation as a scientist. He was important because he alone was able to weave together all that the other chemists knew. He was the first to understand that what others had called "chemistry" was really a disorganized hodgepodge of facts. And only he was able to reorganize chemistry into a science.

Antoine Lavoisier in 1793 while in prison. From an engraving of a
sketch by Mlle. Brossard Beaulieu.

Antoine was tall, slim, handsome, strong and steady as he stood in the courtroom. He believed people trusted and liked him because he was sincere, honest, and had always worked to improve whatever he could.

His countrymen had given him awards for redesigning the Paris street lights, for reorganizing the system they used for mathematics, for making their hospitals run better, for improving the prisons, for making better gunpowder, and for much more.

Grateful French farmers praised him for showing them how to earn more money by growing crops that yielded greater harvests. He had honors from countries all over Europe, and even from America, for his other ideas and discoveries, too.

But now his countrymen were putting him on trial for his life. It didn't help to know that this was because France had a brand new government. Or even that his country had swung away from the idea of a king who had total power in order to become a republic, which was supposed to represent the will of all the French people.

This was the result of a long and very bloody revolution, begun earlier in 1789. The revolution started when Louis XVI tried to raise taxes again. The king was going broke, mainly because he was sending money to the colonies in America to help them win their fight for independence from England. The king wasn't really anxious to help the colonies get free. He hated the British and wanted to see them lose the war.

But the French peasants, farmers, workers and the middle classes didn't care about the Americans' fight for independence. All they cared about was the fact that the king was demanding more and more money from them and

Louis XVI. Painting by Duplessis.

not from the nobles. It all came to a head when the king tried to levy more and higher taxes for one last time.

Then the taxpayers hit back. After four years of fighting, the monarchy was overthrown and France was declared a republic. The king was put in prison, and a new government came into power.

The new leaders began to get their revenge by settling their grudges against anyone suspected of dealing with the ex-monarch. Using courtrooms like this one all over France, they put men, women, even children on trial. Of course, the trials were supposed to be impartial and fair, and the judges were supposed to give everyone an equal chance.

Marie Antoinette, queen of France and wife of Louis XVI, wearing a lavish gown and with the intricate coiffure for which she was famous. Portrait by Madame Vigée-Lebrun.

But as most people knew, the judges were finding so many guilty, that the times were being called the "Reign of Terror." The usual sentence was "death at the guillotine." As soon as the prisoners were found guilty, they were marched straight out of the courtroom, shoved into goat carts, and driven to the executioner to die beneath the guillotine's blade.

That was the kind of trial Antoine Laurent Lavoisier was facing. He and twenty-seven other men were standing in a courtroom in front of a Revolutionary Tribunal, the judges who ran the trial.

The twenty-eight were there because they all owned one business, a corporation called the "Ferme Générale"

Louis XVI, Marie Antoinette, their two children, and the king's sister, Madame Elisabeth, in captivity at the Temple in 1792. Guards stand at the door. For security reasons the family was imprisoned in a thirteenth century dungeon in this building for four months. Engraving on wood.

that had been set up to collect taxes for the king. It was despised because the system the king had set up was so unfair. The owners could keep for themselves any amount over the taxes the king wanted collected.

The twenty-eight owners hired agents who traveled all over France collecting the king's taxes for them. It was well known that the Ferme's tax collectors forced every last sou from the people, whenever they could. Only the king had the power to change the system, or so everyone believed. And so, with the Ferme's way of operating, the rich got richer and the poor got nothing.

In France nobles and clergy, those who could most afford to pay taxes, paid the smallest amount. That left those who could least afford it and they were the ones who had to give the most money. It was little wonder that the common people grew so angry.

Antoine could understand why they wanted their revenge against all twenty-eight owners of the Ferme Générale, and he was finally being forced to face how much he and his associates were hated. Still, he couldn't believe that they meant to do any real harm to him, or to his wife's father, Jacques Alexis Paulze, who was now a very old man. Even though Jacques Alexis Paulze ran the company, he had tried to be honest and fair all his life.

As for Antoine himself he was first a scientist and then

Marie Antoinette on her way to the guillotine in 1793. Jacques-Louis David, who witnessed the procession, drew this pen-portrait of the queen only hours before her execution.

a business man. He couldn't see how the judges could ignore that important fact. With all his heart he was sure the judges would see him as a chemist above all else.

Because he usually kept a cool head, Antoine was doing most of the talking for all twenty-eight. It was natural that he be the leader in the courtroom. Sooner or later he was usually the leader for every group he belonged to.

In the courtroom that morning the three judges, Coffinhal, Denirot and Foucault, sat on a platform, all wearing black coats, black pants, white shirts with starched-stiff ruffled fronts, and black boots. Each judge wore a sash with the red, white and blue colors of the new French Republic across his chest, and a ribbon shaped like a rose on his right hip. Only a judge could wear that rosette.

The public prosecutor was wearing the same outfit, even the red, white and blue ribbons, except for the special

The beheading of Louis XVI on the guillotine.

16

rosette. The three judges and the public prosecutor each wore a high black hat shaped like a long narrow black pipe, trimmed with an enormous red, white and blue feather.

All twenty-eight prisoners were bunched behind a darkly varnished, wooden half-circle railing in the center of the courtroom. The accused always stood, or leaned, on a railing in French courtrooms.

The best seats for the spectators were reserved for journalists, or people that the state wanted as witnesses against the accused, or friends of the new government; but every morning people traveled for miles to watch the trials because they were curious or angry, or because they hated the once rich and nobly born. Admission was free, and there was always the promise of a good show.

Out of the corner of his eye Antoine could see Jean Paul Marat, sitting right up front. Marat was a writer for the newspapers and important to the government. Although he was quiet, Antoine sensed that Marat meant to have a lot to do with the outcome of the trial.

Antoine could also see his wife Marie sitting with the other spectators who had managed to squeeze into the courtroom that morning. It was like Marie to get a seat up front when so many others were turned away.

Small chestnut-haired Marie Paulze Lavoisier had once been very pretty. Now that she was older, she was a good-looking woman who seemed to take in everything quickly and to know exactly what people were thinking. Her eyes were big and round. Sometimes they seemed very dark with just a ring around them, and at other times they sparkled and were almost a deep dark blue.

She must have come there early, sitting since before dawn. Her hands played with a rumpled silk handkerchief.

Antoine loved her all the more, holding her own in the midst of the unfriendly, angry and ragged crowd around her.

Most of the other men's wives were afraid to come to the courtroom. They were safely at home or out of Paris, or even France altogether, but not Marie Paulze Lavoisier. Long ago, Antoine knew, she had learned that you have to face up to what is happening.

As often as she could Marie caught his eye. She nodded at him, smiling bravely as if to show her loyalty and faith. Her smile told him that he could make everything come out all right, just as he often had before. And when he saw her smile, Antoine believed he could, too. Only this time it might be a little harder.

Before the trial began, Antoine decided he would try once again to get the judges to drop the charges. He hoped he could convince the Tribunal to let them all go free. Technically, the "crimes " they were charged with should not have been tried by those judges or by that kind of court.

Antoine believed with all his heart that he was not guilty. "Under the law, you have no power over the charges listed in the Act of Accusation drawn up against the defendants, " he reminded the tribunal. He was sure the judges and the prosecutors knew he was right, but he sensed his protests wouldn't mean anything.

The judges whispered to one another. Antoine still hoped that they would stop the trial, that they would be willing to interfere in what others were calling "the normal procedures of the Republic."

Marat the journalist suddenly shattered the calm in the courtroom. He was the prosecution's star witness. Wildly Marat began to accuse all twenty-eight —Lavoisier most of all—of all sorts of other new "plots."

It seemed obvious to Antoine that Marat had carried a grudge for years and was eager for revenge. The journalist was making up the charges on the spot right then and there. He was acccusing the owners of the Ferme of all kinds of crimes, ending with the very worst crime: ". . . supplying the friends of the ex-king and the old monarchy who were now enemies of the new French Republic with huge sums of money illegally held back from the people."

Antoine, Marie's father and all the prisoners shuddered. That last charge, "money . . . held back from the people," was certain to make everyone furious.

Marat was giving the judges reasons to try the accused as criminals who should be condemned to death.

Finally he was finished.

"You have fifteen minutes to prepare your defense,"the judges sternly told the defendants.

Antoine knew he had to think up a way out of these new charges, and it had to be a very good one. He had to push all his fears away. His life and the lives of the other men, including Marie's father, depended on him. He began to try to prove logically that Marat was lying, but it didn't matter. The judges had already reached their verdict.

"Guilty."

Then they read his death warrant. In part it said, "Antoine Laurent Lavoisier, Nobleman, Member of the former Academy of Sciences, Alternate Deputy to the Constitutional Assembly, former Tax Agent. Living in Paris.

". . . the tribunal, after having heard the Public Prosecutors . . . condemns the above-named to death.

". . . orders that the Public Prosecutor show diligence in having the present judgment carried out within twenty-four hours at the Place de la Révolution of this city and that it be printed, posted and published in all parts of the Republic.

"Done and proclaimed, . . . Year Two of the French Republic, one and indivisible."

The death warrant was signed by all three judges.

All the other owners received the same sentence. Death at the guillotine. As soon as the judges finished reading the death warrant, the prisoners were pushed and shoved toward the goat carts for their last ride to the guillotine. The noise of it all was almost drowned out by the yells and jeers of the spectators.

Antoine shook free of the guards, moved out from behind the railing, and looked up at Judge Coffinhal. He raised his voice, shouting over the commotion. Surely the judge knew he was not an enemy of the people, but a scientist. Would the judge give him a little extra time? Antoine asked. He was working on something important to all of France, a new system of weights and measures. It was a way of measuring that everyone could understand.

"Could I have a few days to complete my work?" he asked.

"The Republic has no need for scientists," Judge Coffinhal snapped.

Lavoisier was executed by the guillotine on May 8, 1794. Marie's father died just a little after that.

Bad news travels fast. The next day the distinguished mathematician Lagrange mourned, "It required only a moment to sever that head, but perhaps a century will not be sufficient to produce another like it."

Two

EVERYONE WHO KNEW him said that Antoine understood the ways of the world. That's why his death at the guillotine was all the more astonishing and shocking to his friends. He was well aware of the dangers around him. It was hard to understand why, during all those years of fighting, he didn't try to save himself and Marie.

But until the very end he never really saw himself in trouble. All his life, it seemed, he had been able to turn things around so that they worked out just the way he wanted them to. And he expected that it would be that way in the revolution, too.

Antoine had always been able to get along, ever since he could remember. Life, school, growing up were pretty easy for him. That was partly because he had a good mind and extraordinary powers of intuition, but also because of his family. His father, Jean Lavoisier, was one of the best lawyers in all of Paris, and both of his grandfathers were lawyers, too.

In fact, from the day he was born, August 26, 1763, it seemed that he was intended for the law. As far back as Antoine could remember, his father would say, "You will be a lawyer. You have the law in your blood."

It wasn't unusual for boys to have their lives planned out for them in that way. What you did for the rest of your life was pretty much set from the minute you were born by the kind of family you were born into. There was a strict class system that spelled out your place in life.

It had mostly to do with the position in society your family belonged to. In those days all of France was thought to be divided into three classes, called "Estates." There were two privileged classes, the clergy and the nobles.

The ruling class, or nobility, was the first order of "Estates." They were the great landowners, whose property was passed down through the family, and most of the wealth and power in France lay in their hands.

The "Second Estate" was the clergy—from the archbishops, bishops and abbots down to those holding lower ranks in the Church. Some clergy were very rich from Church landholdings and from tithes.

Then there was the "Third Estate." That included everyone who was not a clergyman or noble. But there were wide differences here, because this class ranged from the bourgeoisie, which included the richest bankers, shopkeepers and lawyers, to the peasants, who owned almost nothing. The chief burden of paying taxes to the king had always fallen on the third estate.

Even though the nobility and clergy together owned

most of France's farm lands and were well paid with high salaries and pensions, they paid far less than their share of the taxes. Just by using their influence they could usually escape paying very much.

Antoine's family belonged to the bourgeoisie, the middle class that included bankers, merchants and lawyers. For more than a hundred years this group had been growing larger, getting more money and more education. The Lavoisiers had plenty of money. In fact, their house in Paris had windows made of real glass, instead of oiled paper. Only the richest could afford that.

A lot was going on in his father's house while Antoine was growing up. His father's friends included some of the most powerful men in Paris. Some were lawyers, others were bankers, merchants and manufacturers. His father and grandfather were busy lawyers and were highly thought of. They worked for the government and helped to run the city for the king of France, who in those days was still the absolute ruler.

Antoine's father was very important to him when he was a boy. He was five when his mother, Émilie Punctis Lavoisier, died. Soon after, Antoine, his younger sister Marguerite and his father moved to another house in Paris.

It was the same house where his mother had grown up. Her sister, Aunt Constance Punctis, still lived there. From then on she helped his father run their household, supervise servants and take care of his sister and him.

Like many boys from well-to-do families, Antoine had his first lessons at home. The teachers came to his house. When he was eleven, he went to a private secondary school run by the Church. His school, the Mazarin, was one of the best in Paris, and was only for boys of the middle and upper classes.

The Collège Mazarin. Today it is the Institut de France, and houses the Academy of Sciences, among other national academies.

Girls from wealthy families like his sister Marguerite received some education, but they didn't learn the same subjects as boys. Mostly they learned how to embroider, paint, sing or play an instrument, but often they could not read and write.

Students read printed books without any pictures. Illustrations cost too much to put in school books. When the boys studied science they used such instruments as the horseshoe magnet, the thermometer, the chronometer, the reflecting telescope, the compound microscope and the spring balance. These were handmade, but shops selling machine-made instruments were just beginning to open in Paris. The newer instruments were cheaper and sometimes more accurate.

Antoine went to the Mazarin for seven years. By the time he graduated in 1761, he had studied languages, literature, mathematics, philosophy, optics, astronomy, mechanics and chemistry.

Reflecting telescope constructed c. 1749. Conservatoire national des Arts et Métiers, Paris.

Compound microscope, c. 1780. Museum of the History of Science, Oxford.

When he graduated, with his sister, father and aunt proudly watching, Antoine won prizes in language, mathematics and science. He didn't find it hard to do well. Schoolwork came easily to him, just as everything else he did.

Later that same year, Marguerite died. She was fifteen. Though Antoine knew he was expected to hide his feelings, he felt angry and helpless. Yet there was nothing he could do about the silence of her room and the house without her. There would always be a part of him that would be lonely for her.

Deep down, Antoine was glad he was still alive. Sometimes he felt a little guilty about that. Though his Aunt Constance didn't change much after Marguerite's death, he noticed that his father had begun to stay away from home more and more. For the first time since he could remember he was really alone.

Antoine knew he had to do some hard thinking about

just what he really wanted to do with the rest of his life. He knew what everyone expected him to do. But did he really want to go along with their ideas and become a lawyer?

He made himself a promise. For now he would do just what his family planned, but that was only for the time being. He had another idea about becoming a scientist. He wasn't ready to tell anyone about it. Not just yet.

Antoine entered law school just as his father had done. It took two years. In 1763 he graduated and received the degree of Bachelor of Law.

Everyone expected him to take to the law and work hard at being a good lawyer. But Antoine knew that being a lawyer bored him. Science was where all the excitement was.

He believed there were lots of questions about the world all around him that needed answers. He wanted to look for things no one else had ever found. And then he wanted to think about them. He was convinced that the best way to find a new scientific truth was by making systematic measurements and observations. Finally, Antoine decided to change his life's work, to become a scientist and study science. But he realized he would have to go back to school.

He didn't especially like the idea because it meant a lot of extra hard work. But his science classes at the Mazarin had only scratched the surface. So even though he still worked as a lawyer, Antoine started back to school, part-time. Mostly he went to lectures on chemistry and geology at the Jardin du Roi—the Garden of the King—given by Guillaume François Rouelle, the famous chemist-geologist. Although neither teacher nor student knew it, one day Rouelle would be famous for starting Lavoisier off on his career as a mineralogist.

From early dawn until way into the night, Antoine studied anatomy, astronomy, botany, chemistry, geology, meteorology, mineralogy and much more. Minutes were precious to him now. One way to save time, he decided, was not to sit or dawdle at the table at mealtimes. He put himself on a milk diet and drank milk instead of eating a meal.

But his aunt, his father and their friends caught on to him. "Take care of your health because you are wearing yourself out by trying to learn all the different sciences all at once."

And they had a lot more advice, too. "You have a natural taste for the sciences, which leads you to want to know all of them before concentrating on one rather than another."

Then, still later, another of his father's friends stopped to offer even more advice. "Try to concentrate on geology and mineralogy, and also, since it is an indispensable help, upon chemistry." Although Antoine didn't pay too much attention at the time, later this advice would point him in the direction of his life's work. Of all the sciences, he liked mineralogy the most. But chemistry was a puzzle to him, as it was to nearly everyone. Even so, Antoine thought it was important to know chemistry, because it would help in identifying and classifying rocks and minerals.

In the middle of the eighteenth century chemistry was still half fact and half superstition. Chemical experiments were carried out on wooden tabletops in a room that looked more like a kitchen. Chemists used glass containers that were shaped just as they had been for hundreds of years. Most of the time they made their own tools and equipment. Only a very few chemicals could be bought in a shop.

There were no written rules for chemistry. Most scientists didn't know much about the theory of chemistry and didn't have any system to go by. Much of their knowledge had been passed from one chemist to another, and there was little written down.

Chemistry is the science that investigates what the world is made of. Scientists believed that all matter was made of one or more essentially different substances. These basic substances were called chemical elements.

Several thousand years before Lavoisier's time, the ancient Greeks thought about the make-up of the world. They reasoned that chemical elements existed, and that by combining elements, compounds could be formed. As for the elements themselves, they knew about copper, silver, gold, sulfur, carbon, mercury, tin, lead, iron, arsenic, antimony and phosphorus.

From that time on, scientists learned through experiments that one element could only combine with another in certain definite proportions. Still, the way they described their work and why they did it was often unclear. It was a mixed-up combination of magic and science.

When Antoine was learning about chemistry, it was still tied to a strange combination of science and sorcery called alchemy. Many alchemists were trying to turn metals into gold, or to find the magic drink that guaranteed you would live forever, called the "elixir of life."

For Antoine, though, chemistry was important because of the rocks where the elements were found. If he wanted to know more about minerals, he had to learn something about chemistry. But he knew that even with all that extra schooling he was still more a lawyer than a scientist.

Three

ONE DAY IN 1763 his father's friend, Jean Étienne Guettard told Antoine about an expedition that he was planning to survey fields and forests all over France. Guettard was a mineralogist and a botanist. He wanted to make the first geological map of France, which would show the types of soil and all the mineral deposits.

Guettard offered Antoine a job as his assistant. Here was a chance to learn more about science while working for a mineralogist. Antoine couldn't pass it up. Without having any second thoughts he closed his law office once and for all.

Antoine was in a hurry to begin. But he realized they first needed a step-by-step plan outlining what he and

Guettard agreed they would do. No one had ever started a project by setting down all its steps and procedures. It was a new way of thinking about work.

Part of Antoine's idea was to explain their plan to the king and to persuade him to support the expedition. He wrote to the king asking for money and permission to do the project. Usually people waited for an answer from the monarch and would begin only after the king said yes. But, without waiting for a reply, Guettard and Antoine set out, taking their assistants, instruments and servants. They rode their horses from seacoasts to mountains, from the farm lands to cities, busily collecting samples of minerals and earth.

Off and on for the next seven years Antoine and Jean worked on those maps. Eventually they would turn out sixteen maps which would show France's surface features, contours and soil types. But they never did finish Guettard's dream, because the king sent word for them to stop.

Lavoisier and Guettard were disappointed, angry and more. Later they heard that another scientist, Antoine Grimoald Monnet, had picked up from where they left off, using their maps to finish up the project. When the maps were finally published, they were the first geological maps of France, but Monnet never mentioned Lavoisier or all his work, nor did he give him any credit.

But Antoine got a new idea from those field trips. He began to wonder about the mineral gypsum, which was found lying in the fields. It was ground up and used for fertilizer by the peasants and farmers, which made gypsum a very important substance.

Antoine collected it in crystals and chunks until he had several samples. He was curious about it. What was the gypsum really made of? What would it do? What were its properties? He decided to take careful and accurate measurements of the mineral to show its chemical changes.

Antoine believed he could show that there is a logical and orderly arrangement of known facts in nature. He wanted to prove his idea to the older scientists.

He began to investigate what gypsum was made of. He decided that if this method worked, he would take accurate measurements in every scientific investigation. Without knowing it, Antoine was taking a giant step toward one of his greatest scientific works.

Excited by the possibilities, he began his research in the autumn of 1764, while he was still working on other projects. He felt that the old way of finding out about the elements, by burning or heating them, wasn't really telling the experimenters what they wanted to know. He decided to test gypsum by finding out its reactions to a liquid, water. Once again, this was a new idea. He planned to take measurements of his experiments of the water and gypsum and to carefully record what happened in his notebooks.

He tested the gypsum. It dissolved in water. His curiosity pushed him on.

He also found that water made up a part of gypsum. With this knowledge he discovered something never known before. When gypsum was heated, it gave off the water in it and became a powder. Later, when the gypsum powder was mixed with water, it recombined to form a hard plaster.

Antoine was the first to show that the "setting" of gypsum came about because the dry powder absorbed water to form a plaster. Since there was so much gypsum around Paris, he named it, "plaster of paris." From then on plaster of paris would be used for casts, to immobilize broken limbs, for models and for many other things.

Six months after he began, Lavoisier was ready with the results. His findings proved that it was important to use only accurate measurements to describe and predict chemical changes.

Antoine felt his findings were important enough to share with the wisest and most brilliant scientists in all France. These scientists all belonged to the Academy of Sciences. This was an exclusive group that met in Paris to share news of their latest and best discoveries. The Academy was supported by the government, and their collection of scientific instruments was one of the finest anywhere: retorts, mortars and pestles, crucibles, the physicist's concave burning mirror, the astronomer's sphere, a cartographer's map, animal and human skeletons, and much more. Their high standards for science were copied all over Europe.

Membership in the Academy of Sciences was limited to only a hundred and included even the king. It was the very highest honor to be asked to join. Antoine had no doubt that he would be a member some day. Soon, he hoped. The other members had to vote to admit you, and the king himself had to approve your election.

Every scientist sent a report of his important findings to the Academy, hoping to be invited to demonstrate his newest breakthrough at one of their meetings. To be asked to talk about one's work was the highest sign of recognition.

On February 25, 1765, Antoine Lavoisier—a striking figure in his velvet breeches, brocade coat, ruffled shirt and best powdered wig—stood on the Academy's large gold and satin-draped stage. Staring at this young man with some suspicion and doubt were the oldest and most respected scientists in all of France.

Using his flasks, retorts and other pieces of chemical apparatus, Antoine presented everything he knew about gypsum. He repeated the experiments he had done when he found out about plaster of paris. The scientists watched and listened.

He explained that the "setting" of plaster of paris was due to the taking up of water by dry plaster and the combination of the two. He showed what he meant. He demonstrated that when gypsum was heated to drive off three quarters of the water, a powder was formed. And that later, when the same amount of water that had been driven off was added to the powder, you had plaster of paris. Most important, he showed how he measured accurately the water given off. Finished at last, he waited for their verdict.

The members of the Academy agreed that his work was full of new information. "Indeed, it is a remarkable research paper for a chemist who is so young." His explanation of the chemistry of plaster of paris would be included in textbooks from then to this day.

But Antoine had a special reason for presenting his results to the Academy. More than anything, he wanted to be invited to join this exclusive club. When he stood before all these men, describing his research on gypsum, he realized how much he had against him. He was young, without years of experience behind him.

Antoine thought of another way to make an impression on the older scientists. The lieutenant general of the Paris police announced a contest for the best way to improve the city's street lights. The judges for the contest

The Great Burning Lens at the Academy of Sciences. The two lenses A and B concentrated the sun's rays. The substance to be exposed to the concentrated heat was placed on an adjustable support (G). For the protection of his eyes the operator wore dark glasses.

were the members of the Academy of Sciences.

Antoine entered the contest. He planned his project carefully as usual, and made out a list of topics.

He began with the history of lighting the Paris streets. Then he went on to consider all the different ways there were to light a city at night. He showed which of those ways was the best for Paris. He discussed the best type of oil to use for the street lamps, the best shape and the best time to light the lamps. Finally, he showed how they could reuse the oil and how it could be kept from freezing in the winter.

When he was done he was pleased. He was sure he had written up a winner. No one could think up a better plan.

On April 9, 1766, just a month after he had read a second paper to the Academy about the mineral gypsum, Antoine again stood proudly on the large gold and satin-draped stage. He was getting a special award, a gold medal for his brilliant organization of all the information. The president pinned the medal on his coat, kissed him on both cheeks and congratulated him. But he was not the winner.

No one really won the contest. The prize was divided into three smaller awards, one apiece to three manufacturers of street-lighting equipment. However, Antoine's analysis helped the lieutenant general decide on how to light every street in Paris. The city would be safer from then on.

More sure of himself than ever, Antoine decided to apply to the Academy for membership. He felt qualified because he had submitted three great scientific papers and won a gold medal. Besides, he knew plenty of members, who were ready to vote him in, and his father and aunt knew still more.

Later that month, his sponsors added his name to the list of candidates. He was the youngest person ever to apply. Even so, Antoine believed he had nothing to worry about. Whatever he wanted he usually got.

Later, the winner was announced. It was Louis Cadet de Gassicourt. The Academy preferred this older, more established chemist.

Antoine was crushed, but he had another plan ready just in case. He had figured out a way to get around the rules. If the Academy would start a new division, then Antoine Lavoisier could be its first member. He decided to ask his friends to suggest his idea.

But the Academy didn't start a new section. Antoine didn't become a member that year. He sensed he must have shocked the older members, who saw him as fresh and brash.

The next year he tried again. Then, in the spring of

1767, while he was away from Paris on a field trip, he received optimistic news from his father.

"The chances for getting into the Academy in the next election are really excellent."

His family and friends were certain he would be voted in. Antoine was convinced, so convinced, that buying a book in Strasbourg in September, he signed his name in it and added, "Member of the Academy of Science in the year 1767."

But he was wrong.

He didn't make it this time either.

Four

PARIS HAD A water shortage problem, which worried the government. Officials were looking for a better way to increase the water pressure and to pump water in from the rivers.

Antoine saw this as a fresh chance to impress the Academy. Besides, he enjoyed being able to help out where there was trouble. Almost at once he was ready with his plan to pump water into Paris.

Then he went one step further. He showed how the pumped water could be used to put out fires. To show what he meant, he drew up a plan for the officials. It was the first to propose fire hydrants for the Paris city streets. Unfortunately, after all his hard work, the government told him there wasn't any money for either of the projects.

Still, the time Antoine spent thinking about water didn't go to waste. He was making a connection between the work he had done for Guettard on the geological maps and water. It seemed to him that water could be hiding mysteries. Water flowing from rivers, streams and canals could carry a lot of useful information.

"I have to copy nature," he wrote in his notebook, which he kept like a diary. "Water, this almost universal solvent, is the chief agent in shaping the earth; it is the one I have adopted in my work."

It was already known that minerals dissolved in water. If he tested water, would it give him some clues as to which minerals were there far below the earth's surface?

Antoine decided that instead of hauling the buckets of water to his laboratory, he would test the waters right where they were.

He had already used the hydrometer, an instrument used to help measure certain properties of liquids. It could measure how much mineral materials were dissolved in a sample of water. The laboratory hydrometer was too heavy and clumsy to drag around, so Antoine designed a better instrument, a portable model. With this new, light-weight hydrometer he was free to travel anywhere he pleased. Now he could investigate the concentration of elements and the kinds of salts in the waters.

He decided to take a new look at what was already known about water. To begin with, he would test the idea first held by ancient Greek scientists that heat changes water to earth. In Antoine's time, "earth" meant any solid sub-stance.

Ever since the days of the ancient Greeks, people had believed that the elements which chemists took for granted—water, earth, fire—could be changed from one to another. Because of this, many older chemists insisted that water could be turned to earth on a long heating. They also thought that air turned to water and a mist when it rained; wood, if heated, turned to fire, and so on.

In 1768, Lavoisier decided to see for himself what was really happening. He knew that after water was boiled for a long time in a glass container, floating specks appeared. He would boil water for 101 days to see if water really turned to earth, or to any solid substance.

But he was going to add something new to the experiment. He would compare weights. He weighed an empty glass retort. Then he measured an amount of distilled water and poured it into the retort. The retort was heated until the air was largely expelled and then sealed and weighed. Nothing could get in or out.

The boiling went on for 101 days. The water, held inside a device called a "pelican," condensed into water vapor and returned to the flask so that no substance was lost in the course of the experiment.

Specks did appear. He could see flecks of suspended, solid material in the water. Lavoisier wondered if this

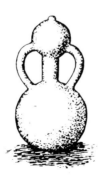

Pelican used for the continuous distillation and redistillation of water. From John French, *The Art of Distillation* (London, 1651).

sediment really did come from the water. To answer the question, he cooled the pelican and its contents and weighed it. There was no change in the weight.

Then he poured out the water and dried and weighed the container by itself. Sure enough, the retort itself was lighter than it had been at the start of the experiment. The weight loss was just equal to the weight of the sediment.

All at once Antoine understood what was happening. The sediment was not water turning to earth at all. It was material from the glass, slowly being eaten away by the hot water, and then showing up as those solid specks. Now he could get rid of that old-fashioned idea that heat converts water into earth.

But the experiment was showing something even more important. Experiments without measurements were useless, and even worse, misleading. Just looking at an experiment wasn't enough to find out what was really going on.

He was sure that many ideas believed for hundreds and thousands of years to be "facts" would now have to change. But the other chemists stubbornly hung on to their "facts" even though they couldn't explain many things. They refused to listen to Lavoisier's new ideas.

Even so, little by little, Antoine's experiments were forcing some chemists to admit that using eyes alone was leading to false conclusions. He was showing that taking measurements was the only way to establish facts. Chemistry was becoming an exact science.

As soon as Antoine's experiments were finished, he wrote a report on what he had done. Once again he sent a letter to the Academy of Sciences telling them of his findings. Then he asked to be invited to share his work with their members.

Antoine could not help wondering how the Academy could keep turning him down as a member. Stubbornly he asked his friends to put his name in one more time. When the messenger delivered the results of the election in the heavy white envelope, he didn't know what to expect.

This time they had voted to admit him. His name had been presented to the king, who had the final say on all members, and the king had also agreed to allow him in.

Now, in 1768, Antoine Lavoisier was finally part of the Academy of Sciences. At twenty-five he was half as old as the next youngest member.

As soon as he joined, Antoine became busier than ever before. Because the king gave money to keep the Academy running, he expected its members to supply him with answers to all kinds of problems about France.

The Academy had committees for almost everything. And Antoine volunteered, it seemed to him, for almost all of them. Some interested him, and some he joined because they were filled with powerful men who might help him. He joined committees investigating the water supply to the city, prisons, the best location for a slaughterhouse, bleaching, gravity, paper, a place to keep gunpowder safely and nearly a hundred other projects.

And, of course, as a member, Antoine could vote "yes" or "no" on others. A few years later, in 1780, he would vote "no" when a journalist, Jean Paul Marat, who called himself a scientist, asked in. Lavoisier, who had a low opinion of his abilities, would turn him down, and Marat would never forget. Nor would Marat ever forgive him. Years later Marat would have his revenge on Lavoisier. It would be a terrible one.

Five

ALTHOUGH HE WAS busy and working hard, Antoine realized he did not have enough money to live on. He was using up the money his mother had left him. Then he even borrowed money from his father to help support himself. Most scientists got money from an outside job, rich patrons or wealthy relatives, but on the whole, they did not earn as much as the lawyers did. Although he had decided not to remain in law, Antoine liked to live as well as if he had.

He knew he needed to find another way to help support himself as a scientist. A few days after he was voted into the Academy, he borrowed money—a half million francs, about ninety-five thousand dollars—to buy part of a business called the Ferme Générale. His father helped him get the loan by guaranteeing to pay back the money if Antoine couldn't. But there wasn't much chance of that. As part owner of the company, Antoine expected to make a lot of money from it.

With Antoine, there were now twenty-eight owners of the Ferme Générale, who paid the king a set amount of money for permission to collect taxes in the king's name. Anything over the amount the monarch asked for the company could keep.

The Ferme Générale collected taxes on tobacco, salt, the grinding of grain, the pressing of grapes and more. All the fruits and vegetables that came in from the farms every morning to Les Halles, the Paris markets just north of the Pont Neuf, were taxed.

France was made up mostly of farm lands. The farmers raised the food and produced whatever else was needed, but they had absolutely no voice in their government. They could do nothing about the amount of taxes they should pay and the kind of goods and services that could be taxed. Or so everyone thought.

To be sure the Ferme Générale would be able to collect everything due them, its owners built gates to the city which were guarded by their collectors. Every peasant and farmer bringing fresh vegetables into Paris had to pay. In many cases the peasant paid the tax even before he sold his crop. Sometimes he didn't make enough to pay the tax, much less bring money home.

The Ferme had hired nearly thirty thousand tax collectors who worked all over France. To run this tremendous business, the owners divided their own work into committees.

Antoine agreed to work on more than one Ferme

Les Halles, 1779. Painting by N. B. Lepicié.

committee at the same time. These jobs were added to all the others from the Academy of Sciences. If he didn't have much time before, he had even less now.

He'd heard that some of the older members of the Academy were doubtful that he could handle so much work. Some scientists were whispering, mostly behind his back. "Can a scientist do two things at the same time?" "How can he devote himself to science if he also runs a business?"

Not everyone was against him. "Antoine's added income makes it unnecessary for him to seek other ways of earning a living. . . . "

"Well, at any rate, he will give us better dinners," argued Lalande, the astronomer.

Never one to do things halfway, Antoine quickly got right into the thick of the Ferme Générale's problems. It was easy for him to reorganize the company so that it ran better than ever; so well, in fact, that he was earning about a hundred thousand francs, or about nineteen thousand dollars, a year from it.

Antoine knew that its director, Jacques Alexis Paulze, was honest and fair, and that he was trying to keep the accounts in order. But he also knew about the bad reputation of its tax collectors, who hid the money they collected and kept it for themselves. Because of these dishonest men, the peasants and the working people were being forced to pay more and more to meet their tax bills.

The cruelty of the tax system troubled Antoine for the next three years. Whenever he could, he traveled to the provinces, not as a collector, but in an attempt to straighten out some of the problems. He discovered that the system could not easily be changed, but he found new ways to organize the collections.

His plans and ideas grew more important to the Ferme Générale, and particularly to Jacques Alexis Paulze. Antoine especially liked to visit him, but not only for business reasons.

The director had a daughter twelve years old, Marie Anne Pierrette Paulze. Marie had fine blue eyes, a small mouth, a distinctly turned-up nose, a clear complexion, (important when so many were pockmarked from smallpox) and pretty auburn hair. She was smart, and her cleverness transformed her face, giving her a thousand different expressions. Antoine found her very attractive.

He knew the gossip about Marie that was being passed around the court and the salons of the Paris rich in 1770. It was said that the Baroness de la Garde, who had a lot of power with the monarch, was insisting that Marie marry her elderly, alcoholic and penniless brother, Count D'Amerval. The reason was obvious. Marie would inherit a lot of money some day.

The Baroness threatened Marie's father that if he did

not agree to her plan, she would see to it that the king fired him from his job at the Ferme Générale. Jacques Alexis Paulze decided that Marie must marry someone else quickly, some handsome and suitable person. Here was his assistant, Antoine Lavoisier, still without a wife. Antoine was overjoyed when Marie's father spoke to him.

As was the custom, her father told Antoine about Marie's dowry, the amount of money she would give to Antoine when they married. Then the two men wrote up their agreement in a marriage contract.

The engagement was announced in November and the contract signed on December 4, 1771. Marie and Antoine were married on December 16. Everyone agreed that it was a marvelous match. Even the Baroness gave her blessings to the couple. By then Marie was fourteen, and her husband was twice as old, twenty-eight.

Antoine and Marie moved into a comfortable house on the Rue Neuve des Bons-Enfants, a handsome side street in Paris. From the very beginning, Antoine and Marie loved each other and were happy together.

Lavoisier was making a lot of money from the Ferme now. His generous pocketbook guaranteed the best for him and his household. Marie carefully supervised their servants. She made especially sure that the cooks in the kitchen created wonderful dishes.

Soon their dinners were famous, not only for the food, but for their guests, too. These included the American Quaker Benjamin Franklin, idol of fashionable women and the only man without a powdered white wig at the king's court; Gouverneur Morris, the United States Minister in Paris who negotiated the price the Ferme paid for Virginia tobacco; DuPont the politician; the Duc de la Rochefoucauld, a generous patron of science and leader of many liberal movements; and the Duc de Chaulnes, who once entered a closed cabinet in which charcoal was burning to study the effects of gas and was pulled out and revived by his personal servant. If there were foreign scientists in Paris, they were certain to be invited: James Watt, the great British inventor, or Felice Fontana, the Italian famous for his research on snake venom.

The Lavoisiers had guests almost every night. Marie spent a lot of time making certain their home had the most fashionable colors—a medium or dark tan called "buff," or a lighter, brighter yellow called "chamois"—and the finest furniture.

Many fourteen-year old wives were running large households in Paris, but Marie wanted to be a lot more than a good hostess and an efficient homemaker. She decided to do something which was considered most unusual for a woman at that time. She made up her mind to work alongside her husband, and to help with his chemical experiments at the laboratory.

Lavoisier's English wasn't very good. He couldn't read or write it easily, so Marie began to teach herself that difficult language. Soon she could both read and write English and was translating reports from other scientists into French.

With Marie's help, Antoine learned what other chemists were doing, especially Joseph Priestley and Henry Cavendish from England, and Karl Wilhelm Scheele of Sweden. All three men were experimenting with gases, a subject which interested Antoine more and more.

Later, when she was nineteen, Marie decided to learn still another foreign language, Latin. The ancient alchemists

Joseph Priestley.

had used Latin, and many chemists of the 1770s still used it, too. Since most researchers began projects by reading whatever was already known about the subject, which was usually written in Latin, Marie decided to learn the language to help Antoine.

Marie wrote to her brother Balthazare and asked him to teach her. He was a linguist, writer and traveler who knew Latin well. Soon she could translate chemical data from Latin into French.

She also took art lessons so that she could illustrate

Henry Cavendish. He was the first scientist to fully describe hydrogen and to discover the chemical composition of water. Drawing by Alexander.

Antoine's books and reports about his experiments. One of their closest friends was Jacques-Louis David, a brilliant painter. David took time away from his own paintings of Paris life to teach Marie how to sketch, paint and engrave. Later David would paint a portrait of Marie and Antoine, the only one ever done.

Sometimes it took as long for Marie to illustrate one of Antoine's experiments as it took for him to do the work. Although there were plenty of books, thanks to the printing press, illustrating a book was slow and expensive.

First Antoine designed specially squared paper for Marie to use in the illustrations. A paper-maker in Paris made up the sheets just as Antoine told him to. With these squares on the paper, Marie could make drawings that were accurate and showed every detail of Antoine's careful experiments.

Marie began each illustration by making freehand watercolor sketches. Then she copied the sketches in accurate detail using pencil. They were made on the squared sheets of paper, which were exactly the size of the finished book.

Then Marie painstakingly transfered each completed drawing via waxed paper onto a smooth copper plate, using a sharp cutting tool. She cut the design into the copper so that the ink rested in the hollows, and she wiped off the ink on the surface. Carefully, she pressed each plate on paper and added the lettering to it.

She marked each plate "Bonne," meaning "good," then added "Paulze Lavoisier Sculpsit." Repeating each step thirteen times, she produced thirteen different illustrations.

That was the practical side of her art lessons. But she loved to paint. Whenever she could find free time, Marie put something on canvas. Often she asked a visitor to pose. She particularly liked to paint Benjamin Franklin, the American envoy to the Court of Versailles. Franklin, who was famous as a scientist, was in Paris to get French money and supplies and win friends for America.

Franklin and Marie talked while she worked on the canvas. Franklin told her about the colonies' desire for independence from England and about what life was like in America. Marie understood what it meant to try to break away from an established system. Everything she did—learning languages, chemistry, even knowing how to read

Benjamin Franklin crowned by Liberty. Aquatint by the Abbé de Saint-Non, 1778.

and write—was different from what was expected of women. She found that exciting.

Marie and Antoine loved the letter Franklin wrote in thanks for her gift of the finished portrait. He took it back with him all the way to Philadelphia, Pennsylvania. "It . . . is allowed by those who have seen it to have a great merit as a picture in every respect, but what particularly endears it to me is the hand that drew it."

As busy as they were, the Lavoisiers always liked to try something new and different. But when Antoine received still another command from the King, it seemed that he might stretch himself too far. The King chose him because "Antoine was . . . well known for his work in chemistry, his technical ability, integrity and capacity exhibited in his work in the Ferme Générale."

The monarch ordered Antoine to become a commissioner of gunpowder. He was to be one of the four commissioners in France in charge of making ammunition. This was a very important duty because wars could be won or lost on the quality of the gunpowder used on the battlefield. It was an honor that Antoine could not refuse.

Antoine saw that there was still another way he could serve the king and his country. He got ready for the job by designing a new method of preparing potassium nitrate, called saltpeter. When saltpeter was mixed with sulfur and charcoal, it produced gunpowder. Antoine made it easier to collect and use the chemical and even to make the ammunition itself.

Although this job was important to France, Antoine couldn't know at that time that it would one day also mean a lot to the Americans fighting for independence. Within a few years, he and Benjamin Franklin would exchange favors. First Lavoisier asked Franklin, an expert on electricity and lightning rods, to help him design new blastproof warehouses for the royal gunpowder and saltpeter stores. Franklin agreed to design the lighting devices for the arsenals. Now Lavoisier owed Franklin a favor.

Sometime afterwards Franklin called in that favor. During the American Revolution, George Washington's troops were desperate for gunpowder. Franklin was in Paris mostly to try to buy saltpeter from the French. But French officials didn't want to sell because saltpeter was also valuable to them for their own gunpowder supply. The French officials couldn't stop Franklin from buying the saltpeter. Instead they refused him the export permits needed to load the saltpeter on ships sailing from the Paris docks.

Then Franklin turned to Lavoisier, who found a way to help out. As Director of the Gunpowder Arsenal Lavoisier would use his influence and order small amounts of saltpeter to be loaded onto many different boats sailing from Paris. He got export permits for these small amounts. The ships that reached George Washington brought him enough saltpeter for his gunpowder supply. So Antoine Lavoisier's new job would one day help the cause of the American Revolution.

Six

ALTHOUGH THEY WERE pleased to be chosen by the king, Antoine and Marie weren't too happy with what went along with the honor. As Director of the Gunpowder Arsenal Antoine was expected to live right above the gunpowder factory. In that way, the king reasoned, Lavoisier could oversee the mixing of the gunpowder and look after the royal saltpeter and gunpowder stores.

In 1775 Marie and Antoine watched their servants and assistants carefully load their furniture, clothes and laboratory equipment onto wooden wagons. Their belongings were pulled through the narrow, crowded Paris streets to their new home while they followed in their coach.

The damp old arsenal appeared gloomy and grim, but

Antoine and Marie were excited by the prospect of changing everything in the director's apartment to suit them.

To begin with Antoine wanted a new laboratory for chemistry experiments. He was determined to make it one of the best anywhere. He planned out every detail of the new, large private laboratory, making sure he had lots of room for all his experiments. As usual, before he began, he made long, careful lists and then made complete, precise drawings of what he wanted. He ordered new equipment, the finest he could buy from the best instrument makers in Europe. He spared no expense. When he had finished, his laboratory was soon known as the best equipped in all of Europe.

Marie wanted the best for their new home, too. She ordered furniture of velvet and brocade and gold, and many satin draperies. Their apartment was one of the most magnificent and elegant in that elegant city of Paris. Marie and Antoine would live there happily for more than sixteen years. They were bright, handsome and talented, and they had many good friends.

More scientists and statesmen than ever came to their laboratory and apartment above the gunpowder arsenal, which were famous even as far away as America. Some guests were happy just to watch Antoine, Marie and their assistants perform tests and experiments. Many students who were fired with ambition to become chemists also visited. They were just as welcome as the better-known visitors. Often Antoine would loan them money, or he used his influence to find them jobs.

All of this cost a lot. A scientist always had bills to pay, and Antoine's experiments and his equipment were expensive. He had to pay for the chemicals, supplies, implements, tools, machines, his assistants' salaries and much more.

Then he had to have a huge amount of money for their expensive life style. He needed far more even than he was making as a commissioner of gunpowder, but his connection with the Ferme Générale gave him the added income they needed.

He and Marie enjoyed being able to live in their magnificent apartment and offer dinners of the finest wines and foods to visitors and friends. As Gunpowder Commissioner there were many state occasions where Lavoisier had to do his share of celebrating.

For instance, in December of 1778, a cannon boomed over Paris to announce that Queen Marie Antoinette had given birth to a girl. The king ordered a free distribution of wine and bread. The Corps de Ville, the municipal officers, paraded around a bonfire. All public buildings were illuminated at night. Then, at the Place de l'Hotel de Ville, the City Hall square, wine, bread and sausage were passed out again. The people rejoiced. As good loyal subjects Marie and Antoine gave a party at home. Still, at their apartment and all over Paris they heard whispers: "What a pity this baby was not a boy. . . ." But a little prince was to be born later.

It was even more important to Antoine that he could use the money from the Ferme Générale for his work. He could afford to buy the best chemicals, hire assistants and continue with his research.

He could also afford to buy a chateau, a country house with farm lands, outside of Paris in 1778. He and Marie often traveled by coach to their farm in the countryside at Fréchines in Blois. He was very interested in farming, and his ideas about agriculture were as new as his ideas about science. He set out to establish a model farm.

He wanted to prove to the farmers, at his own expense, that they could earn more money when they used his new ideas about growing crops. Sowings and yields were weighed, fertilizer was measured, crops were rotated. He drew up reports on cultivating flax and a "new" vegetable called potatoes, helped improve the breed of sheep, and did much more for the peasants living on his farm land.

Antoine kept exact, double-entry records for every expense and every receipt, for each field under his care. He kept a set of records at Fréchines and another set at Paris. His ideas about farming were so successful that in 1785, the king set up a new committee on agriculture, with Lavoisier as its head. Even George Washington, living in Virginia, far away across the Atlantic Ocean, wrote asking news of Lavoisier's new farming ideas. Washington used them on his own farm, Mt. Vernon.

Antoine cared about his farm and the peasants on it as much as he cared about everything he was involved in. When the townspeople of Blois suffered ruined harvests and severe famine in the disastrous summer of 1788, Lavoisier sent them generous amounts of money to buy wheat for the starving. These were loans without interest.

"Lavoisier," the farmers said, ". . . is a great and good man who saved our farming district." The grateful townspeople of Blois made him an honorary citizen.

There was still another way he helped all the farmers. His idea would last from then on. Because of his efforts, the government used a system that guaranteed old-age pensions for farm workers. Peasants and farmers could invest small sums of money and be guaranteed an income when they were old.

In Paris, life above the arsenal was also bustling. Ministers of state came to ask Antoine all kinds of questions—nothing seemed too small or too large for him to consider.

They asked his advice on food for prisoners, on the sanitary conditions of the hospitals and prisons, on the paths of bullets, on how the ships at sea could get fresh water from saltwater, on the best design for wheelchairs, on how to spot counterfeit money, and on how to go up in a balloon and come down safely. Often Antoine had to pay his own expenses to find the answers. Still he kept adding projects.

Antoine knew he also had to stay in touch with other scientists in foreign countries to find out what they were doing. That took up a lot of time. With Marie's help he sent letters to the French provinces as well as to governments all over the world. And of course, he also went to the Academy of Sciences' committee meetings.

The Lavoisiers did all this by planning their time. As practical as he was in everything else, Antoine scheduled everything they did. Just as he organized science, he also organized their life.

They got up every morning before six and ate breakfast. Then they went to the laboratory for precisely three hours and Antoine did his experiments.

For the rest of the day he was a statesman, businessman, financier, organizer, farmer and committee member all rolled into one. There were committee meetings of the Ferme Générale, the Academy, state officials, or else preparation of reports or inspections of gunpowder factories or visits to hospitals or checking of the Ferme Générale's accounts.

Every evening friends, visiting scientists and students arrived, and they all would return to the laboratory. Sometimes a scientist wanted a behind-the-scenes look at La-voisier's latest project. If a guest wanted to help, he was assigned a part in the experiment.

It was Lavoisier's rule to try out every new experiment on a group of friendly scientists before presenting his conclusions to the Academy. He didn't like to leave any-thing to chance. The world around him often asked for his advice and sometimes sent him medals or ribbons of honor, but he steadfastly kept on with his new ideas for science.

Seven

THE YEARS PASSED. Marie and Antoine were busy all the time with experiments, new scientific ideas, trips and meetings.

Letters from scientists arrived from all over Europe. From letters and from Antoine's talks with other chemists, he and Marie knew many chemists were interested in how things burned in air. All agreed that fire and the nature of combustion were important, but their explanations of what was taking place were mostly just guesses. The problem was that it was difficult to measure gases. Animal bladders were used as containers for the gases, and they were hard to work with and to handle. Still, many scientists were already studying the effect of heat and fire on all kinds of materials.

This wasn't new to Lavoisier. Off and on he'd been doing experiments in this area since 1772.

More and more he realized that he was returning to the work of other scientists, in particular to those puzzling questions about the "phlogiston" theory. The phlogiston theory had been shaping their experiments for almost seventy-five years. It said that all substances contain phlogiston, which is liberated on burning.

Chemists also used "phlogiston" as a sort of handy, all-purpose ingredient to explain all sorts of chemical reactions. Still, one of the main uses of the phlogiston idea was to explain what they observed in experiments that had to do with burning. Depending on the experiment and the explanation the scientist needed, phlogiston could have weight, be weightless, or even exhibit what was called "negative weight."

Across the channel in England, Antoine knew, the famous English clergyman-scientist Joseph Priestley was insisting that fire was the freeing of that mysterious element called "phlogiston."

The usual explanation given by Priestley and the other scientists was that metals and other easy-to-burn substances, such as phosophorus or sulfur, contained an invisible substance called phlogiston. The reason why a substance crumbled to ash when it was burned was that phlogiston had "departed" from it.

This all seemed foolish to Lavoisier. He didn't believe in "phlogiston," and he didn't believe any explanation using it amounted to anything. It was annoying to see the other chemists hanging on to this idea. And, even if the other scientists did agree with Priestley, Lavoisier thought Priestley's idea was just ridiculous.

Precision balance, c. 1770. This particular balance was constructed for Henry Cavendish. Royal Institution, London.

Still, he knew his hunch about fire and burning and phlogiston was not going to be enough to change anyone else's mind. Not just yet. He would have to do experiments in his laboratory and then record and classify facts before he could find out more about fire.

The other chemists were quite content with their phlogiston story. Still, Antoine suspected that if he took careful and accurate measurements while experimenting with heat and burning, he would find some completely new answers.

In some ways he was going back to those earlier days when he used rocks and minerals in his experiments. Only now he wasn't so much interested in finding out about ores and metals for themselves as in what happened to them when they burned over charcoal.

For instance, when he burned phosphorus and sulfur in the laboratory, he could prove that they weighed more after burning than they did before. He suspected that something had been gained from the air.

Yet most of the other chemists read these same experiments and results differently. They insisted that the added weight came because phlogiston went from the charcoal to the phosphorus and the sulfur.

Antoine wrote in his notebook: "Chemists have made an imaginary principle out of phlogiston which, not strictly defined, fits all explanations required of it; sometimes it has weight, sometimes it has not; sometimes it is free fire, sometimes it is fire combined with earth; sometimes it passes through the pores of vessels, sometimes they are impenetrable to it."

One of Lavoisier's very best friends, the chemist Pierre Joseph Macquer, didn't waste any time replying: "Mr. Lavoisier frightened me for a long time with the surprising discovery which he has carefully kept to himself and which seems to overthrow the phlogiston theory. His assurance quite upset me. Where would the old chemistry be if we were forced to rebuild it completely? I, for one, would have forsaken it. And now, Mr. Lavoisier brings his discovery into the open and I assure you that it gives me a sinking feeling."

Lavoisier shot back, "I do hope that my ideas will be adopted at once; the human inclines to one mode of thought and is slow to change."

But in spite of his reputation as a scientist, Antoine was alone in this fight. Only Marie stood by him. Still he went ahead. He didn't doubt for a minute that somehow he could prove he was right.

He started a series of experiments with precisely weighed quantities of tin and lead. His tests wouldn't be done in the casual way chemists usually worked when they said something like:

You take a little of this and . . .

. . . You take a handful of that.

. . . You take a big flask. Or a small tube.

. . . You heat near boiling, but not hot enough to boil. . . .

For the first time he used specially made balances, more accurate than ever before. One of them could measure a weight change as small as a hundredth the weight of a drop of water.

With those accurate balances, he used precisely weighed quantities of tin and lead. Both burn at lower temperatures than many other metals.

When these two were heated in a closed container with a limited supply of air, a thin film of rust appeared. Chemists called this thin film a "calx."

Both metals formed this calx on the surface. The calx was the ash which remained after metals and minerals had been thoroughly roasted or burned. Oddly enough, after that thin film of rust appeared, no more rust formed. The odder fact was that the rust-coated metal weighed more than the metal did before it was heated.

This was all a curiosity to the chemists, but it wasn't

new. And, it certainly wasn't startling. The chemists had an explanation for the added weight. "The rust weighs more because 'phlogiston' is lost from the metal and added to the rust," they said. And they thought this showed why the calx was known to be heavier than the metal it replaced.

But as he measured and worked, Lavoisier was sure he would find a different explanation for what was happening.

Taking a precisely weighed quantity of tin, Lavoisier first placed it in a retort, sealed it and made it air tight. He weighed it and heated it until no more of the powdery calx was formed. He reweighed the flask. There was no weight change.

Then he broke the seal, allowing air to rush in, and took the exact weight of the flask again. This time he found a weight increase. Later he would understand that this was because the tin was reacting with the air in the flask.

For the moment, though, he believed that the evidence showed that the calx was made up of a combination of the metal with air, and that the rusting didn't involve a loss of phlogiston but a gain of at least a portion of the atmosphere. Now he understood that the calx formed when the tin became hot enough to begin to combine with the air.

Finally, he concluded, the weight increase was due to the weight of the air rushing in when the flask was unsealed. And this weight had replaced the weight of air originally in the closed apparatus-which had just been used up in forming the calx.

He wasn't really sure just what had been removed from this "air." He just described "it" as some "atmospheric principle." Later he would be able to tell what "the atmospheric principle" was.

The world of science seemed completely hostile to his discovery. Yet Lavoisier would not stop demanding that chemists throw out the phlogiston theory once and for all. He knew that he was asking a lot. But as he saw it, the facts were there, proven by his experiments.

But no chemical work of any importance, even one written as late as 1799, so much as mentioned this set of experiments or Antoine Lavoisier's theory about "phlogiston." The other chemists ignored it.

Eight

EVEN THOUGH THE other scientists were ignoring his theory, Lavoisier kept on with his work. A few years earlier, on February 20, 1773, he had written in his laboratory notebook that he would do a project on gases. More than anything, he wanted to make chemistry an exact science. Yet he didn't expect that this particular set of experiments would be the one to do it for him.

From Marie's translations he already knew about the two British chemists, Priestley and Cavendish, who were working on gases. In 1766, in England, Henry Cavendish had discovered a gas which he called "inflammable air." In those days gases were called "airs." Our atmosphere was known to be a gas, but at the time this was all going on, chemists didn't know that our atmosphere was a mixture of several gases.

Lavoisier also knew that in 1774 Priestley and Cavendish were working together in England to develop a way to collect and store gases. Their new method was now making possible a serious study of gases.

Then in October 1774, Joseph Priestley came to Paris. Priestley stubbornly believed in the phlogiston theory. The English scientist used it to explain all he found out in his experiments.

Soon after he arrived, Priestley was invited to have dinner with the Lavoisiers and a group of other scientists. They traded information. All of them were having trouble in distinguishing between different kinds of "gases."

Priestley told how by heating a red calx of mercury he got a gas in which a candle burned much more brightly than it did in ordinary air. Priestley called this gas "dephlogisticated aire," because everthing burned more quickly in it. He spoke of this new "aire" many times more while in Paris. He reported that when he took a deep breath of the gas, he found that he felt "much invigorated." But in spite of all his experiences and experiments, he could not identify the gas.

Lavoisier began to think back to his own work. He had already experimented with heat, fire and gases, too, and he knew the "red precipitate of mercury" well. Priestley had been unable to prove the exact nature of his new gas, but Lavoisier believed he could pick up where Priestley had stopped. He decided to repeat Priestley's experiments under the most careful conditions to see what else he could find out.

Joseph Priestley sailed back to England and returned to

Method devised by Joseph Priestley for collecting gases over mercury, 1772-74. New "airs" or gases that were soluble in water were discovered. Today we know them as hydrogen chloride, ammonia, and sulfur dioxide.

his laboratory. He also wanted to repeat the experiments. The two chemists were both working on the same problem. They were looking hard at the same experiments, but Priestley saw one thing, Lavoisier another.

Priestley didn't waste any time. He had a new sample of the red precipitate which he had bought in Paris to repeat his earlier experiments. Since he believed in phlogiston, he decided that it had something to do with the gas he was finding.

After more tests he separated the captured gas once again. He was more convinced than ever that his "dephlogisticated aire" was a new gas, "between four and five times as good as common air." He meant that it felt good when he inhaled it. He said, "it had a beneficial effect on the lungs."

As soon as he could, he published news of these experiments. Then Joseph Priestley may have smiled to himself. He believed his interpretation was right. He was ahead of Lavoisier in the race.

In France, Lavoisier heard what had happened. He learned that Priestley had recovered the portion of air, or that part which had converted mercury into the red rust. He was upset and very disappointed that he had missed an important discovery, the most important link in his whole chain. He went back to his laboratory all over again.

Lavoisier had a hunch about Priestley's new gas. He believed that it was identical to the vital part of ordinary air, the part needed for breathing and for burning. He set to work, using a simple experiment to prove his point.

He confined mercury and air together in a retort and heated it gently in order to produce mercuric oxide—the red powder Priestley had used. Lavoisier found that the formation of the mercuric oxide went on for twelve days, then stopped. Since the supply of mercury in the retort was not used up, Lavoisier concluded that the gas—which was necessary for the formation of the red oxide—had been all used up.

As he repeated the tests, he realized at once the "key" to what they were both doing. But his conclusion was very different from Priestley's "Dephlogisticated aire." Lavoisier recognized that only a part of air was combining with mercury.

Then he found that the mercury had risen one fifth of the way into the space formerly occupied by the air. From this Lavoisier reasoned that one fifth of the air was a gas that could combine with mercury. Lavoisier understood for the first time that only a part of the air was combining with the metal, and that the air and this single gas were quite different. He found that the gas was "different, more respirable, therefore, purer than common air."

This was one of his most important discoveries. Lavoisier called this gas "oxygen," from the Greek word meaning "acid-producing." He chose the word carefully to

The glass vessels in which Joseph Priestley first isolated oxygen in 1774.

be sure that no one would ever confuse this new substance with "air" again.

Antoine went on to name the rest of the air, the other four fifths which could not support combustion. He called that part "azote," from the Greek word meaning "no life." After some years "azote" would be changed to "nitrogen." Chemists all over the world would use the word nitrogen, except in France, where it is still called azote.

He told his assistants, "Air is not a simple substance, but it is a mixture of two or more gases." One fifth of the air was oxygen and four fifths was azote.

Later, Lavoisier put together what was happening. He made a connection between the two kinds of actions: breathing and burning. After all, he reasoned, "We breathe in air rich in oxygen, but breathe out air that is lower in oxygen." He experimented with expired air, breathing out. It produced less mercuric oxide. Lavoisier had proven that Priestley's "perfect air" and the vital one fifth of ordinary air were identical—the gas oxygen. All in all, as Lavoisier saw it, this was the knockout punch to the idea of phlogiston, once and for all.

Meanwhile, on the other side of the Channel, in England, on March 23, 1775, Priestley read a letter to the British Royal Society announcing his discovery of a new gas. He was first. He had beaten Lavoisier's announcement to the French Academy of Sciences on April 26, by one month.

Not wasting a minute, Lavoisier hurried to get news of his discovery written up quickly. In May the *Journal of Physics* carried news of his findings.

Priestley was waiting to publish details of his work in a book. Of course, this took longer. When he took time off to read what the *Journal of Physics* told about Lavoisier, he grew more and more furious. He could not find the slightest mention of his own name. Lavoisier was claiming all the credit for himself.

Vowing to have the last word, Priestley rewrote parts of his book. He called careful attention to the many "mistakes" he said Lavoisier had made. He also told of their conversation in Paris.

There was no doubt that Priestley was accusing Lavoisier of stealing his discovery, of taking the credit for himself. And from then on, Priestley would tell this to anyone who would listen.

When Priestley's angry accusations reached him, Lavoisier thought hard, but not for long. Even though Priestley hadn't understood the true meaning of his own work, the real truth was that Priestley, not Lavoisier, had discovered oxygen. Lavoisier had picked up what Priestley had missed. He had named it, understood it and pointed out its importance. He could claim credit for everything but finding oxygen.

Yet, it was that last bit of credit that Lavoisier wanted the most. He wanted it for the pleasure and thrill of discovery, but also for the honor the world of science always gave to the person who found the new element. Even though he would do more for chemistry than any man before or since, he never discovered an element of his very own.

Lavoiser was willing to offer a half apology to Priestley for trying to take all the credit. Still he couldn't bring himself to give up every shred of the claim to the discovery of this new gas. He definitely considered Priestley a tinkerer in the laboratory. And he hated to take back his claim.

Grudgingly, Lavoisier wrote in 1782, "This aire which Mr. Priestley discovered at very nearly the same time as I and I believe even before me. . . ."

No one could argue that he, Antoine Laurent Lavoisier, had named oxygen. He understood it, and he pointed out its importance to nature. He alone showed with his precise experiments and careful measurements that oxygen is absolutely necessary for something to burn, that combustion is a chemical reaction, and that air itself is a mixture of gases.

His findings about elements sparked still another new project. One that would one day bring him the name, "the Father of Chemistry."

Nine

Lavoisier could see chemistry was beginning to change, but too slowly to suit him. Besides, there still was a wall between him and the other scientists.

Although people came to him for all kinds of advice on other subjects, he still had to convince chemists to go along with his new ideas. Yet, he was more sure than ever of what he was doing. Only materials that could be measured or weighed or reactions which could be observed by others offered facts worthy of the science of chemistry.

It seemed a good time for change. Not only in science, but in a lot of other ways. For one thing, people were beginning to question what was going on with their government. Some of their questions were sparked by the treaty signed in Paris on September 3, 1783, by the British, the Americans and the French, which ended the American Revolution.

It was all the more sweet to sign that peace treaty in Paris, because King Louis XVI, who hated the British, had spent a fortune helping the Americans win that war. The king had declared a national holiday. There were prayers of thanksgiving for peace. The king ordered free wine and sausages to be given out to the people. There was dancing in the streets. Thousands of toasts were drunk to that new, young country across the Atlantic Ocean, and to its Revolution.

And while they were celebrating, many French people realized that the Americans had stood up to the king of England against what they believed to be an unfair tax system. Until now this had been an unthinkable idea.

Now the French people were beginning to change, too. They were questioning their own taxes imposed by the king, especially since the chief burden of paying taxes was falling on those who were getting so little.

Lavoisier wan't afraid to speak out against what was going on. He sent articles to the newspapers on all kinds of topics. Often his stern judgments and sharp pen didn't make him liked by either the rich or the poor. Now he was unpopular because of a controversial issue, the newly built wall surrounding the city of Paris.

For years people had tried to sneak fruit and vegetables into Paris without passing through the tax gates. Almost one fifth of the produce was smuggled in that way. Merchants complained bitterly about the smuggled produce sold at a much cheaper price. The shopkeepers were losing a lot of money, and the nation was losing a lot of taxes.

Above: the apparatus used to accomplish the decomposition of water; *below:* the recomposition of water. The experiment was conducted in 1785. Despite the mounting political furor that led to the French Revolution a few years later, Lavoisier still managed, while fulfilling his many other duties, to continue his scientific experiments at the Arsenal Laboratory.

Finally, the Ferme ordered a wall built around Paris with only a few openings, all well guarded. The idea was to build a simple high wall so that the Ferme Générale's tax collectors could inspect every carriage, coach and wagon coming into the city.

But the contractor that the Ferme Générale hired went too far. He built a luxurious ornamented stone barricade with elaborate gates and fancy trimmings. It was very expensive. The city was shocked. Both rich and poor complained, "The wall cuts off the pure air and makes it harder to breathe." "The Ferme Générale has put the whole city of Paris into a prison."

Before he knew it, Lavoisier found he was being blamed for the whole costly mess. An unsigned pamphlet read, "Everybody thank Lavoisier as the patriot to whom we owe this ingenious imprisonment of the capital."

This "Paris wall" story would be used against him one day when he least expected it, by the journalist Marat, who carried a grudge against Lavoisier. Marat would never forget that he had lost his chance of election to the Academy because of Lavoisier's vote against him. Now he had a double grudge to settle. And when times changed still more, he would see what he could do.

By now, 1785, Lavoisier was Director of the Academy of Science. As its Director, Lavoisier had still more duties. Somehow he managed to squeeze everything in—building his new foundations of chemistry in his laboratory, carrying on his work to raise better crops out at his country farm, and running the powder commission, the Academy and the Society of Agriculture. He submitted more than fifty reports on subjects that ranged from how to keep cider from spoiling to the natural history of Corsica. This work was asked for by the king and his ministers. Then he edited still more reports that carried other people's names.

At the King's request he took the time to study where the criminals and the sick were kept. He knew the Paris prisons could be improved. But the hospitals really distressed him. He shuddered as he entered, shielding his nose from the stench, his eyes from the view. Only the very poor went there or were carried there or dragged in.

They lay in massive, old wooden beds, five or six feet across, five people of mixed sex and age to a bed. To save space, the feet of one patient rested against the head of the next. In the same bed lay those with burning fevers,

1er Mars 1785. (Cotte B)

On a pesé le globe de Verre où s'est faite la Combustion des deux airs et où l'eau resultante de cette Combustion s'est deposée. on l'a Suspendu au Bras droit de la Balance de M. Lavoisier avec son harnois de fil de Cuivre et une plaque de Verre blonde qui en Couvre l'ouverture.

il pese — 1 ℔ ... 4 on. 2 Gros ... 17 gns
tare — 0 ... 14 on. 5 Gros 34 ½ gns
poid de l'eau — 0℔ ... 5 onces 4 Gros ... 54 ½ gns

Le poid de l'eau formée dans le Ballon est de cinq onces quatre gros cinquante quatre grains et demi. cette eau étoit parfaitement transparente et sans couleur et avoit un gout très Sensiblement acide; elle rougit la teinture de tournesol et le papier qui en est teint, et ne precipite point la lune cornée. les commissaires presens sont convenus d'une assemblée subsequente pour verifier la tare du ballon et pour d'autres objets à constater Definitivement. à Paris ce 1er Mars 1785.

Le Duc de la Rochefoucauld   Jay   Cadet
Bailly   Laplace

on a repesé les tubes de verre pleins d'alkali deliquescent après l'operation.
tube numero 2 avec bouchons, faveur, alkali et cotton — 9 onces 4 Gros 45 grains
avant l'experience — 9 onces 4 Gros 0,75

augmentation de l'alkali ou l'air inflammable à passé 0 on 0 Gros 44,25 grains
quarante quatre grains un quart

le tube numero 1 ayant été cassé par le col, on a soigneusement recueilli tous les morceaux, et l'on a trouvé son poids comme il suit
Verre, Bouchons, filette, cotton et alkali — 9 onces 2 Gros 56 grains
avant l'experience — 9 onces 2 Gros 20,75
augmentation de l'alkali ou l'air dephlogistiqué — 0 onces 0 Gros 35,25
à passé trente cinq grains un quart

Meusnier

One sheet from the record of the experiment resulting in the decomposition and recomposition of water. At the bottom of the sheet can be seen Lavoisier's signature, among those of others. March 1, 1785.

scabbed skin, measles, broken arms and legs, smallpox, tuberculosis and other contagious diseases. Lavoisier suggested some changes on running the hospitals, but the plight of the patients seemed almost beyond help.

He was doing what he could to improve the quality of life for the good of the people. But Antoine's work as a scientist always came first.

Around that time one of his friends, Guyton de Morveau, was trying to write about chemistry for an encyclopedia. De Morveau was having a hard time trying to explain the different ideas about chemistry, old and new, because each chemist seemed to use different words to express the same idea. Also, they all had to unlearn all they had been taught about phlogiston, and get rid of its old-fashioned language.

He asked Lavoisier to help him with his assignment. Antoine agreed. As usual, Antoine thought and planned before he acted.

He saw that chemistry needed one logical language that would say the same thing to all chemists no matter what other language they used—French, German, English, or Swedish. The future of chemistry depended on a common language for all chemists.

Antoine decided to invent a new system in which every substance would have a name based on what it was made of. Every substance on earth, Lavoisier believed, was either a single element or a combination of various elements in certain proportions. His system would show how all the different substances related to each other. And it would get rid of the phlogiston theory once and for all.

Lavoisier submitted a memo to the Academy of Sciences, "Reflections on Phlogiston." It hammered away at the old-fashioned notions and set down Lavoisier's ideas:

1. Each phenomenon could be explained in terms of oxygen.
2. Explanations using phlogiston were complicated or absurd, or both.
3. Oxygen could account for *all* changes. Oxygen could explain everything phlogiston could with less confusion.

But when he introduced all this to the Academy, the other chemists didn't like his ideas. Most of them couldn't understand what he was talking about. And what was worse, when he tried to explain, most of them wouldn't listen.

Ten

Just as if he were planning a battle, Lavoisier drew up a plan to introduce his new system, showing how all the different substances related to each other. It was going to take a huge amount of time.

Pierre Simon de Laplace, the famous astronomer and mathematician, was the first in the Academy to volunteer to help. Still, the chemists hung back.

Eventually, one chemist, Louis Berthollet, offered to help after announcing that he felt Lavoisier was correct. A year later, Antoine de Fourcroy and Guyton de Morveau followed. This team of four chemists was what he needed.

Soon the four were called, "the French Chemists." They worked together with Antoine and Marie to develop their new system. It would be a complete break with the past in that it would describe substances according to their characteristics and behavior. Their method was based on Lavoisier's new theory that scientists should define ideas precisely and clearly. For instance . . . "An element is the last point that chemical analysis is capable of reaching."

To identify each element, they searched it out and tested it for themselves. They added better definitions to make it easier to understand what the chemist was talking about.

Part of their system was to give information about the proportions. They used endings such as "-ite," "-ores," "-ate," etc. Each of these indicated how much of an element was in something.

In the summer of 1787, the four published a three-hundred-page book, *Méthode de Nomenclature Chimique,* *(Method of Chemical Nomenclature).* They divided the book into two parts.

The first, and by far the larger and more important part, overhauled the language itself. There were new and simpler names for chemical substances. It included a dictionary which listed first the new name, and then its old name. In the second part, the new name was arranged in alphabetical order with the old name next to it.

Although de Morveau had originally had the idea to clean up the language of chemistry, Lavoisier organized, combined and restated chemists' discoveries so that it all worked as a single scientific system.

As soon as its fame spread, the *Méthode de Nomenclature Chimique* was read all over France. There were translations for chemists from other countries, too. The book contained information about thirty-three substances that the chemists

A contemporary drawing which asks the question whether Priestley was a politician or a priest. A pastor as well as a scientist, Priestley's liberal religious views won him many enemies in England. In 1791 a mob angered by his views demolished his laboratory but failed in its attempt to burn down his house.

thought were elements. Even though we now know they were wrong in some cases, it was a real breakthrough.

Still, like many other ideas that are new and different, the new book was looked at with distrust and suspicion. A few chemists even laughed at it.

Priestley, in England, stubbornly refused to go along. As a matter of fact, for the rest of his life Priestley would fight to keep the idea alive that phlogiston was the basis for chemistry as a science. He would never stop insisting that oxygen was "dephlogisticated aire." He would shut his eyes and turn away from any findings or facts that might shake his faith in that old-fashioned theory.

Following on the heels of *Méthode,* Antoine published a book of his own. It was called the *Elementary Treatise on Chemistry* and appeared in 1789. The engravings Marie made so carefully were used as illustrations. With this book he finally laid the foundations for chemistry as an exact science. One by one, chemists began to accept his new

TRAITÉ
ÉLÉMENTAIRE
DE CHIMIE,
PRÉSENTÉ DANS UN ORDRE NOUVEAU
ET D'APRÈS LES DÉCOUVERTES MODERNES,

PAR M. LAVOISIER.

Nouvelle édition, à laquelle on a joint la Nomenclature Ancienne & Moderne, pour servir à l'intelligence des Auteurs ; différens Mémoires de MM. Fourcroy & Morveau, & le Rapport de MM. Baumé, Cadet, Darcet & Sage, sur la nécessité de réformer & de perfectionner la Nomenclature Chimique.

Avec Figures & Tableaux.

TOME PREMIER.

A PARIS,
Chez CUCHET, Libraire, rue & hôtel Serpente.

M. DCC. LXXXIX.

Title page, *Traité Elémentaire de Chimie* (*Elementary Treatise on Chemistry*), 1789.

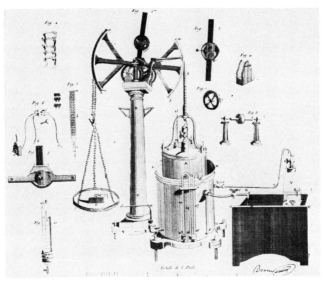

A copy of the final proof of Plate VIII from *Traité Elémentaire de Chimie*. To show that a plate met her exacting standards, Marie Lavoisier would scratch the word "Bonne" and her initials in the lower-right-hand corner.

system, but very slowly at first. Lavoisier had brought about a revolution in chemistry.

But that was not the only revolution getting started. Despite his feeling good about his book's success, Antoine was growing worried about the world outside his laboratory.

The winter of 1788–89 was a time of hardship for everyone, especially the poor. There was less and less money left to run the country. France's treasury was really bankrupt, and the king had even drained his own personal bank accounts.

Then the king called a meeting of France's richest men, 145 of his chief nobles, bishops and officials. Louis XVI asked them all to agree to a new tax, this time for the privileged classes. They refused. The Third Estate, the

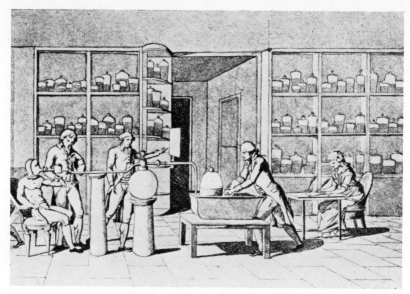

A copper plate drawing by Madame Lavoisier showing her husband performing a metabolism experiment at the Arsenal Laboratory, c. 1789. At the left the young scientist Armand Seguin breathes oxygen through a brass mask. The main point of this experiment and similar ones was to learn how much oxygen the body used for various activities. At the right Madame Lavoisier takes notes.

people who always paid, would have to pay all over again.

But the Third Estate was having an especially bad time. There were poor harvests. Grain prices were sky-high. Jobs were scarce, and there were fewer ways to earn money. People were starving. If a worker did have the money for food, he could buy only three quarters of what he had bought just a few years earlier. The lower classes were hungry, fearful and very angry.

Later in the spring of 1789, the king held a meeting at his palace at Versailles. Representatives of all three estates were invited, but things became worse.

In a few weeks, by June 17th, representatives of the Third Estate saw more taxes and even higher prices coming. Their group, disgusted and impatient, proclaimed itself a new and different "National Assembly." The Third Estate invited the other two Estates to join the "National Assembly" to work out a way together to help out France. But only a few nobles and clergy joined them.

Then the king locked the new "National Assembly" out of their meeting hall at Versailles. Furious at being shut out, their leaders led the group to another palace building nearby. It was large and was used as a riding hall or tennis courts. There were fiery speeches from the leaders. All the representatives of the Third Estate took an oath. They would not leave until they had written up a new constitution for France. This historic pact came to be called the "Tennis Court Oath."

News of what was going on at the king's palace spread from Versailles to Paris and to all of France. In early July another rumor swept Paris: the King was bringing his

"The Tennis Court Oath," by Jacques-Louis David. June 20, 1789.

troops to Versailles to overawe the Assembly. This was the last straw. People began to fight the king's army in the Paris streets. Shops were looted. Royal officers were attacked. And yet, no one really accepted the fact that the fighting would grow into a real revolution, certainly not one which would spread quickly, overthrow the king and change all of France forever.

In spite of all the unrest, Antoine and Marie were still caught up in their own exciting lives and their own plans for the future. There was fighting all around them. The royal fortress prison, the Bastille, was around the corner from their gunpowder works. When the head of the Bastille, Launay, lowered the drawbridge to admit some artillery of the king's Royal Guard, the crowd rushed in. Every prison guard was killed. The fall of the Bastille was a sign that the people were behind the Assembly. That was July 14, 1789.

The storming of the Bastille on July 14, 1789.

A new spirit of freedom surged through Paris. Then it swept through France. The old regime was crumbling fast. People suddenly realized that they could get rid of the monarch and his unjust laws. Lavoisier, however, believed that the remedy was to remove the injustices.

From then until 1792, the radical antimonarchists were in control. For more than three years, one group after the other seized power. Finally, France was declared a republic. Local officials were to be elected by the people, and a new system of courts with elected judges was set up. Testing freedom and power, the people began to hunt down the hated tax collectors.

Antoine felt that, after all, he was first a scientist, and his chemistry was the most important part of his life. Many wealthy nobles and clergy were leaving France in fear and to protest what was happening. Lavoisier didn't seriously consider these possibilities. It seemed to him that he, Marie and his father-in-law were perfectly safe.

Eleven

By 1793, INSIDE the gates of Paris the fighting was turning out to be a very bloody revolution. Signs all over the city called for "Blood of the Aristocrats" and "A Free and Democratic Government." Everyone was drawn into the war. Workers, farmers, peasants and revolutionaries were struggling to overthrow the armies of King Louis XVI.

There was hand-to-hand fighting in the city's cobblestone streets, on its steep slate roofs. There were clashes along its tree-lined boulevards and beautiful gardens. The battles had spread outside the city's gates to the countryside, the fields, the forests and even to the king's own hunting parks.

Members of the aristocracy were all considered the enemy. They were killed for being who they were. In three years of war, thousands of men, women and children were hauled off to die at the guillotine.

Yet, Antoine and Marie weren't afraid. They were waiting out the war in the heart of Paris with the skirmishes going on all around them. They could have left if they had wanted to, but Antoine was convinced that they were safe.

Besides, he was doing his best for all sides of the fighting. He was helping to keep the hospitals open for the wounded, to keep the schools open for the children, to get fresh food delivered to Paris every day and much more.

Antoine could get along with almost everyone. He could see both points of view. As a farmer he understood firsthand why the peasants and workers were so angry. He agreed that changes were needed in the French government. Perhaps he didn't realize that he was being marked for death by some of the very people he was trying to help.

With Marie working beside him, Antoine continued his experiments during the revolution. The pair were working on many new scientific discoveries such as a new system of uniform weights and measures which would one day be called the metric system. While they worked, they tried to shut out the battles outside the thick brick walls of their apartment. They tried not to hear the screams of the men, women, children, magistrates and even rival revolutionaries being carried off in goat carts among the angry screaming mobs to the scaffold.

Even when friends from as far as America sent them letters begging them to leave while they could, the Lavoisiers reassured them that they were safe. The pair did their scientific research, helped run Paris and waited out the war.

But neither Marie nor Antoine had any idea of the strange events that were taking shape, events that would involve them in the most unexpected way.

Twelve

THE DAY THE Committee for Public Safety came into power spelled real trouble for the Lavoisiers.

The Committee was part of the new government that could arrest people, put them on trial and sentence them. The police, the judges and the jury all belonged to the group that was in power. If the Committee ordered your arrest, it usually meant you were automatically found guilty, and they forced you to leave the country, put you in prison, or put you to death. And most often the sentence was death at the guillotine.

Now, newspapers carried stories about the Lavoisiers that were both unfair and untrue. Many were written by Jean Paul Marat, the writer with a grudge against Antoine.

LE COMITÉ

DÉ SALUT PUBLIC

DU DÉPARTEMENT DE PARIS

A SES

CONCITOYENS.

LES prédictions sinistres des assassins de la Liberté s'accomplissent.

Le défenseur austère des Droits et de la Souveraineté du Peuple, le Dénonciateur de tous ses ennemis, Marat dont le nom seul rappelle les services qu'il a rendus à la patrie.......... Marat vient de tomber sous les coups parricides des lâches Fédéralistes. Une Furie, sortie de Caen, département du Calvados, de la maison du ci-devant comte d'Ovet, a plongé le poignard dans le sein de l'apôtre et du martyr de la révolution.

Citoyens, du calme et de l'énergie, et surtout de la surveillance........ l'heure de la Liberté a sonné, et le sang qui vient de couler est l'arrêt foudroyant de la condamnation de tous les traitres...... Il scelle à jamais l'union intime de tous les patriotes qui vont sur la tombe de ce grand homme jurer de nouveau la Liberté ou la Mort.

MARCHAND, *Président.*

HARNY, *Secrétaire.*

De l'Imprimerie Patriotique et Républicaine, n° 355, vis à vis l'Assomption.

A Committee of Public Safety poster.

His articles mainly stressed that Lavoisier was an owner of the hated Ferme Générale. Many people forgot Antoine's generous and good deeds, or his scientific breakthroughs. Now he was attacked at public meetings because he was part of the king's old government.

At about the same time, the schools, clubs and com-

Jean-Paul Marat. This portrait by Boze was painted in April 1793, at a time when Marat was active at the proceedings of the Revolutionary Tribunal.

mittees he belonged to were closed. Finally, even the business he owned, the Ferme Générale, was shut down, too.

By now, in 1793, there was fighting between the revolutionaries and the government, and fighting among the revolutionaries themselves. The trouble was that the laws kept being changed. Everyone, it seemed, wanted more from the new government, and it promised more than it could deliver.

Antoine and Marie had lasted it all out. But the morning of September 10, 1793, was to change their luck, and lives, forever. On that eventful day, agents of the revolution pounded on the door to their apartment, shouting, "We're here for a search."

CHAPTER TWELVE

Helpless, the Lavoisiers watched the agents of the revolution look for evidence that would give the slightest excuse for an arrest. They dumped stuff out of drawers, threw books from the library shelves, broke apart furniture, scattered papers and records, and destroyed the research in the laboratory. But the searchers found nothing.

The next day Marie and Antoine were forced to watch all over again as the agents came back to finish tearing up the apartment and laboratory. The searchers were determined to uncover a reason to arrest them.

Lavoisier believed that he could depend on his reputation as an important, famous scientist to help them through. But, on a snowy, blustery December 24th, Antoine and Marie heard about a new order from the Revolutionary Committee. This one called for the immediate arrest of all the owners of the Ferme Générale. Antoine knew he couldn't trust his luck any longer.

The Lavoisiers and their servants grabbed what they could. They rushed down a long flight of back stairs, and just as the agents of the revolution arrived, they escaped.

Finally, they reached one of the great forests surrounding Paris. From his hiding place Antoine sent a message to Paris. He asked the Revolutionary Committee to take back its order for his arrest. It replied: "Give yourself up, or we'll come and get you."

Antoine faced one of the most important decisions of his whole lifetime. His life and Marie's depended on it. Finally, he decided. He would show he was not afraid of the agents of the revolution. He would give himself up.

Their coach and horses slipped quietly back through the gates of the city, through the narrow, cobblestone, back streets with their old, tall, beautiful houses. Marie and

243 Boulevard de la Madeleine, where Lavoisier arranged to live after leaving the Arsenal in 1792. The sophisticated and well-equipped laboratory at the Arsenal was taken apart and never reassembled.

Antoine knew that this was the end of the life in Paris that they had always known.

The city was clear and cold. Marie and Antoine saw it now with different eyes. They ignored what they had once loved, the bare trees sculptured against the sky, the gardens, the winter wind whistling across the surfaces of the ponds and the fountains.

When they returned to their apartment, Antoine gave himself up of his own free will. As he was marched away to the prison, Antoine kept telling himself that things would come out all right. He was not an enemy of the people, he was a scientist.

Thirteen

THE SNOWS OF January and February began to melt. The drenching rains of March and April ended. It was springtime, 1794, with its flow of clear, sparkling days. With the good weather, the revolution's bloody fighting grew even more fierce.

Antoine and the other Ferme Générale owners had been locked up in the Bastille prison all winter long. It was a hard winter for all of them. Especially for Antoine's father-in-law, elderly Jacques Paulze. Even though Marie's father was an old man, the jailers showed him no mercy. He was one of the owners of the Ferme Générale, and that was reason enough to treat him roughly. The revolutionaries hated all the aristocrats. Often, they would drag any aristocrat caught on the street off to prison.

A goat cart taking the condemned to the guillotine.

Their cruelty was felt the most in Paris. The times were called "the Reign of Terror." Thousands of Royalists and aristocrats were put to death, and so were the Committee's rivals in the scramble for power.

But still the Committee tried to show that they were doing everything according to the laws. They used the Laws of Suspects to arrest anyone who was an "aristocrat" or who was "suspected of disloyalty to the Republic." Then they had the Revolutionary Tribunal, a court where arrested people stood trial, were condemned to die, and were then hurried off to the guillotine.

And so the "lucky" ones were shoved into prisons which were filled to overflowing. Families, friends and other visitors came to see the accused, bringing food, blankets, clothes and whatever else the prisoners needed to stay alive.

In the Bastille, Lavoisier wasn't letting the time slip by. His important work on the metric system was near to being finished and printed. Séguin, one of his still loyal assistants, came from the print shop every day carrying page proofs.

Lavoisier wanted to finish the metric system and his book, *Mémoires de Chimie (Memoires of Chemistry),* as quickly as he could. His private hope was that Marie, her father, their friends and he could still manage to ride out the storm. Looking at the thick walls of his cell, Antoine could have felt that the prison seemed lonely and far away from the rest of the city, from his former life, as he listened to the moans, coughs, cries and weeping of the prisoners.

Then one day a rumor swept through Paris. Finally it reached him in prison.

"The Ferme Générale adds moisture to the tobacco they sell," went the whispers.

Moisture made the tobacco heavier, and since people bought tobacco by its weight, the buyers were being cheated. "And what is more," the gossips added, "the smoker's health is threatened by inhaling the wet tobacco."

The "report" gave the Committee for Public Safety the excuse it needed. They ordered all owners of the Ferme Générale to stand trial before the Revolutionary Tribunal. In those times it meant the same as a sentence of death.

Early on the morning of May 7th, Antoine, his father-in-law and other members of the Ferme Générale were questioned over and over again. All that day, Antoine tried to convince the questioners that the stories about the wet tobacco were all false rumors. But the questioning kept on and on and on, even through the night.

Just after midnight, a copy of the newest charges was shoved at each prisoner. The writing was smeared and almost illegible in the candlelight that flickered in their dark, damp cells.

As daylight filtered through the bars of their cells, their jailers marched Antoine and the others upstairs to the courtroom. The group squeezed behind the courtroom's half-circle wooden railing.

Antoine could see, peering down from their platforms, three of the sternest judges of the revolution: Coffinhal, Denirot and Foucault.

Though some of the others were losing hope, Antoine still believed he could explain away the rumors to the judge.

The courtroom grew hot, noisy and crowded. By ten o'clock, the prosecutor, jury and witnesses were all in place. It was the moment they all dreaded. The trial began. . . .

Antoine's training as a lawyer years ago when he was younger came back to him. It was just what he needed. As usual he took charge right away.

"Under the law you have no power over the charges," he began.

But Antoine would not be able to change the outcome of the trial. The same man who had been able to make chemistry into an exact science would not be able to change the minds of the three judges.

Their sentence would be carried out immediately: ". . . death at the guillotine."

Fourteen

MARIE WATCHED HER husband and her father executed by the guillotine. They died within a few hours of each other. Soon afterwards, she became a fugitive from the revolutionaries, too. The people in power saw her as one of the hated aristocrats. She was the daughter of one owner of the Ferme Générale, and the wife of another.

She tried to slip away from Paris to safety. But she was caught, brought back and imprisoned in the Bastille.

Shut up in that stone fortress, she discovered that she and Antoine had mostly fair-weather friends. In spite of all the favors she and her husband had done for others, there was almost no one willing to offer her help now that she needed it.

Through it all Marie stubbornly insisted that she

would survive. More than that, she promised herself that she would not let people forget her husband Antoine Lavoisier, nor his brilliant work in chemistry.

After Marie was released from the Bastille, people advised her to try to rebuild her life. Even as she did, Marie knew she would never be the same. She'd lost the men she loved above all: her father and Antoine.

Yet, in spite of all her sadness, she knew she must continue to complete Antoine's last work, the *Mémoires de Chimie*. She had to make his ideas, experiments and writings live forever.

As soon as she could, she went back to his writings. She was especially worried that a few chemists, knowing that Antoine was no longer able to stand up for his rights, would claim credit for his work.

She set down chemical formulas, experiments and conclusions just as Antoine had taught her to. She used all her training as a chemist to pull his work together and correct the mistakes. If she had a question, she had to work out the answer for herself. Antoine, her teacher and guide, was no longer there for her to turn to. Finally she wrote an introduction to the *Mémoires de Chimie*.

Soon other chemists began to realize that Marie was able to translate very complicated scientific work accurately from foreign languages into French. Some scientists were surprised because it was so unusual for a woman to be this well informed about science. They saw that Marie knew what should happen in a chemical experiment. She could pick out the errors and point out mistakes in the most complicated chemical equation.

When the *Mémoires de Chimie* was finished at last, she could not bring herself to try to sell the book to a publisher. Instead, she published it herself and sent free copies to the most famous scientists in Europe, England, even the United States. After they had read her husband's work, there could be no doubt. No other chemist could claim any of Antoine's research or ideas.

And then, there was a complete turnabout of feelings about her husband. Two years after the revolution, the heads of the new French government erected a statue of Antoine Laurent Lavoisier and placed it in Paris. It was little consolation to Marie.

When the revolutionaries returned almost all of the money they had taken from her, Marie used it to try to go on with her life. She lived in Paris almost as well as she and Antoine had before the revolution. But she would never forgive her countrymen for what the had done to her father and her husband.

From then on it was difficult for Marie to trust anyone. She handled her business affairs herself, and now made all her decisions about her fortune. Choosing carefully, she used her money to help the families of the men in the Ferme Générale that had been executed. She was generous to the few servants who had tried to shield her from the revolutionaries and who had tried to help her during the war years. Then, she also gave money to one of Antoine's favorite charities.

Many men wanted to marry the good-looking and intelligent widow. Eventually she married the American Benjamin Thompson, Count von Rumford in 1805. The two had known each other for four years and traveled together all over Europe. Yet, within the first two months, their marriage turned out to be extremely unhappy, a disaster. Later they were divorced.

Although Marie lived until 1836, her happy life seemed to have stopped with Antoine's death. They had had a special relationship, and no one else could ever take his place.

She did live to see the world honor Antoine as the father of modern chemistry. It recognized that his work had helped to bring chemistry out of the shadowy, half-magic half-truths of the Middle Ages and turn it into an exact science.

Lavoisier's *Elementary Treatise on Chemistry,* published in 1789, was the first time chemical principles were pulled together. Eventually he was looked up to by chemists for classifying many of the chemical names and terms that scientists would use. From then on students would study chemistry as a single scientific system.

His passion for exactness in measurements was his key to the new chemistry. He understood how important it was to use balances, and to weigh chemical elements and compounds exactly before and after reactions. He designed new laboratory equipment that made it practical to weigh gases. He helped set up a uniform system of weights and measures which is called the metric system.

Lavoisier gave oxygen its name and made it the cornerstone of modern chemistry. When he searched out the properties of oxygen, Lavoisier threw out the mistaken idea of phlogiston for good.

And while he was doing so much for science, he was helping people in lots more ways, too. His agricultural ideas are still used all over the world. He helped to set up new systems for taxes, banking and money.

It seemed he could find ways to make changes for the better in almost everything he touched and worked with. The work of Antoine Lavoisier, chemistry's founding father, would live on with everyone who ever wondered about the world.

Appendix

The *List of Elements* compiled by Lavoisier, which appeared in his
ELEMENTS OF CHEMISTRY.

TABLE OF SIMPLE SUBSTANCES.

Simple fubftances belonging to all the kingdoms of nature, which may be confidered as the elements of bodies.

New Names.	Correfpondent old Names.
Light	Light.
Caloric	Heat. Principle or element of heat. Fire. Igneous fluid. Matter of fire and of heat.
Oxygen	Dephlogifticated air. Empyreal air. Vital air, or Bafe of vital air.
Azote	Phlogifticated air or gas. Mephitis, or its bafe.
Hydrogen	Inflammable air or gas, or the bafe of inflammable air

Oxydable and Acidifiable fimple Subftances not Metallic.

New Names.	Correfpondent old names.
Sulphur	
Phofphorus	The fame names.
Charcoal	
Muriatic radical	
Fluoric radical	Still unknown.
Boracic radical	

Oxydable and Acidifiable fimple Metallic Bodies.

New Names.		Correfpondent Old Names.
Antimony		Antimony.
Arfenic		Arfenic.
Bifmuth		Bifmuth.
Cobalt		Cobalt.
Copper		Copper.
Gold		Gold.
Iron		Iron.
Lead	Regulus of	Lead..
Manganefe		Manganefe.
Mercury		Mercury.
Molybdena		Molybdena.
Nickel		Nickel.
Platina		Platina.
Silver		Silver.
Tin		Tin.
Tungftein		Tungftein.
Zinc		Zinc.

Salifiable fimple Earthy Subftances.

New Names.	Correfpondent old Names.
Lime	Chalk, calcareous earth. Quicklime.
Magnefia	Magnefia, bafe of Epfom falt Calcined or cauftic magnefia
Barytes	Barytes, or heavy earth.
Argill	Clay, earth of alum.
Silex	Siliceous or vitrifiable earth.

Lavoisier's List of the Elements, which appeared in the *Traité*. The
work was translated into English by Robert Kerr and published in
Edinburgh in 1790.

Index